COUGAR HUSBAND AND OTHER STORIES

KIM MATOS

Humans are mysteries

MELANIE WEBSTER

CONTENTS

INTRODUCTION

This book is an interesting love story about a woman who never knew the true identity of the man he married and other stories.

CHAPTER I

Cougar Husbandry

It was just a normal morning. Almost exactly five years ago. I was making tea in the kitchen. Bobby was still in bed. And we get this knock on the door. I opened it up slowly, and saw the police standing there. At first I wasn't worried. We had this crazy lady that lived next door, and the police were always checking up on her. So I assumed they had the wrong address. But the moment I opened the door, twelve officers came barging past me. Some of them had 'FBI' written on their jackets. They went straight back to the bedroom, and walked up to Bobby. I heard them ask: 'What's your name?' And he said, 'Bobby Love.' Then they said,

'No. What's your real name?' And I heard him say something real low. And they responded: 'You've had a long run.' That's when I tried to get into the room. But the officer kept saying: 'Get back, get back. You don't know who this man is.' Then they started putting him in handcuffs. It didn't make any sense. I'd been married to Bobby for forty years. He didn't even have a criminal record. At this point I'm crying, and I screamed: 'Bobby, what's going on? Did you kill somebody?' And he tells me: 'This goes way back, Cheryl. Back before I met you. Way back to North Carolina.'"

✳ ✳ ✳

"Back in the day my name was Walter Miller. It was a pretty normal childhood. We grew up poor, but nothing really dramatic happened until I went to a Sam Cooke concert at the age of fourteen. I was excited to be at that concert, so I pushed my way to the front row—right near the stage. The crowd was really moving, because it was dance music. And Sam Cooke didn't like that. He kept telling people to sit down. And after only two songs, he got so angry that he walked off the stage. So I screamed at the top of my lungs: 'Sam Cooke ain't shit!' And in North Carolina, back in 1964, that was enough to get me arrested for disorderly conduct. Things went downhill pretty quick after that. My mother was raising eight kids on her own, so she couldn't control me. I got into all sorts of trouble. I lifted purses from unlocked cars. I was stealing government checks out of mailboxes. I got bolder and bolder, until one day I got busted stealing from the band room at school. They shipped me off to a juvenile detention center called Morrison Training School. I hated everything about that place. The food was terrible. The kids were violent. I still have scars from all the times I got beat up. Every night, while I was falling asleep, I could hear the whistle of a freight train in the distance. And I always wanted to know where that train was going. So one night, when the guard turned his back to check the clock, I ran out the back door-- toward the sound of that whistle. And that was the first place I ever escaped from."

* * *

"I followed those train tracks all the way to Washington DC. And for a minute, it seemed like everything would be alright. My brother lived in the city, so I started sleeping at his place. I enrolled in a new high school. I was going to class. Playing a little basketball. Things were going smooth. But I hadn't learned my lesson yet. My old ways caught up with me, and I fell in with the wrong group of kids. These guys were robbing banks—and getting away with it. So I decided to tag along. We'd drive down to North Carolina because those banks had less security. And we got away with it a few times. After every score, we'd hang out on the strip at 14th and T, and act like big timers. We felt like gangsters. I have nobody to blame but myself. I just enjoyed the feeling of having money. But the fun didn't last for long. Because one of those banks had a silent alarm. And while we were stuffing our bags full of money, the manager pulled the trigger. The police were waiting for us in the parking lot. All hell broke loose. I tried to get away, ducking and weaving, running through cars. But I got shot in the buttocks. The bullet went right through me. I woke up in the hospital-- with a hole in the front and back of my coat."

* * *

"It was all over for Walter Miller. The judge sentenced me to twenty-five to thirty years. I held out hope for awhile. I was doing appeals. I kept hoping to win on a technicality, or at least get a new trial with a better lawyer. But I kept hitting dead ends. And reality soon set in-- I was going away for a very long time. They sent me to a maximum security facility called Central Prison.

Gun towers and everything. There was no way out, so I sorta got used to it. My mama died during this time, and that really shook me up. Because my entire life she'd been praying for me to turn my life around. And she never got to see it happen. So I committed myself to doing better. I became the perfect inmate. I never had a mark on my record. My behavior was so good that they transferred me down the hill to a minimum security facility. This place was more like a camp. They still had gun towers and everything, but there was a lot of freedom. They let us walk around the yard. We could make phone calls. I even had my own radio show. It was a lot of fun. I recorded it every Wednesday, and they played it on the local college station. I was relaxed. I was feeling good. I had no plans to escape."

* * *

"Everything changed for me when someone screamed 'punk ass' at the prison captain. He was walking through the parking lot. It was early in the morning, and it was still dark, so he couldn't see who did it. I was working in the kitchen, so there was no way it could be me. But the captain said that he recognized my voice— and he wrote me up. After that he started picking on me. I tried to keep my head low. But the more I tried to do good, the more I got punished. He wrote me up for all kinds of phony things. He accused me of stealing a newspaper. He accused me of faking sick. The negative reports kept piling up, until I was one mark away from being sent back up the hill. And that's when they started putting me on the road. It was the worst job in the prison. They'd call your name before sunrise, and you had to get on this bus. Then they'd drive you all over Raleigh to clean trash off the highways. It was awful. People would be throwing hamburgers and milkshakes at you. And it was almost winter, so it was starting to get cold. That's when I started planning and plotting. I saved up my money. I memorized the bus route. I noticed that we always stopped at a certain intersection—right next to a wooded area.

And I figured I could make that distance in no time at all. I also noticed that the guard who worked on Tuesday never searched the prisoners as they boarded the bus. So one Monday night, while we were watching the Colts game on TV, I made the decision. That was going to be my last night in prison."

* * *

"I cleaned out my locker before I went to sleep. I wanted to leave nothing behind. No phone numbers. No addresses. Nothing they could use to find me quick. Because I worked at the radio station, I was allowed a single pair of civilian clothes. I put those on beneath my prison garments and wore everything to bed. I didn't sleep a wink that night. Every three hours the guards did a head count, and I kept seeing that flashlight shine on the wall. When the sun finally came up, I jumped out of bed and splashed water on my face. Then I glanced out the window. The careless guard was stationed at the gate. The one who never patted down the prisoners. So I said: 'That's it, I'm leaving.' I got on the bus and went to the very back row, right next to the emergency exit. It was a five minute drive to the wooded area. As we slowed down for a stop, I swung open the back door-- and I was gone. I could hear the alarm blaring behind me, but I didn't look back. I peeled off my green clothes and just kept running. The sweat was coming off me. I looked like trouble, so I did my best to keep out of the white neighborhoods. Every time I passed a brother, I asked for directions to the Greyhound station. Everyone kept telling me: 'Keep going, keep going, keep going.' When I finally got there, I found a brother in the parking lot who agreed to buy me a one way ticket to New York. I waited until the last minute. I jumped on the bus right as the driver was closing the door. Then I slunk down in my seat while we drove out of Raleigh. Once we got on the highway, the girl next to me started making small talk. She asked me my name. I thought for a moment, and said: 'Bobby Love.' And that was the death of Walter Miller."

* * *

"Bobby Love arrived in New York in late November, 1977. I was glad to be free, but I was still in a tough spot. I had to build a life from scratch. All I had was $100 in small bills, a single pair of clothes, and a brand new name. I moved into a fleabag hotel, and for two weeks I survived on hotdogs and marijuana. Then my money ran out and I started sleeping on the trains. I had to figure out a way to get a foothold in life. I wasn't even a person. I had no papers, no ID, no nothing. Believe it or not, the first thing I got was a social security number. I walked up to the window and told the lady a story about losing everything, and she gave me a card. On the spot. I still have it today. Next I got hold of an original birth certificate, scratched out the name, and typed 'Bobby Love' on the line. Then I took it to a print shop and copied it so many times that it didn't look fake anymore. It didn't take me long to find a brother at the funeral home who agreed to notarize it. He wouldn't sign it, but he'd stamp it. And that was enough for me-- because I found a brother at the DMV who pretended not to no- tice. And that's how I got my drivers license. Then I used all my new papers to get a job working in the cafeteria of the Baptist Medical Center. And that's where I met Cheryl."

* * *

"Cheryl was innocent. The opposite of me. And that's why I was so attracted to her. I never wanted to date someone like myself: who drank, and smoked, and had a past. Cheryl was soft. Almost naïve in a way. I never told her about my history, and she didn't really press me. I did tell her that I grew up in the South-- which was true. And that I'd come to New York City to try something new. That was true too. But I never told her about Walter Miller.

I didn't see the need. Walter died a long time ago, on that Greyhound bus out of Raleigh. I was a new man. I was Bobby Love now. And if that was enough for her, why complicate things? We got married in 1985. Time went by. We raised four children together. I just couldn't risk it. My family in North Carolina kept telling me: 'You've got to come clean. You've got to tell her.' But they didn't know my wife. Not like I did. Cheryl is a righteous woman. Most people, when they see a dollar dropped on the street, will put it in their pocket. But not Cheryl. She will stop everyone on the sidewalk, looking for the owner. She's that kind of woman. And that's not the kind of woman who could keep a secret like this. I'm not trying to say that she'd have called the cops on me. But she'd have made me call the cops on myself. She'd turn up the heat. So I just couldn't tell her about Walter Miller. And there was no need. Bobby Love didn't have a criminal record. Bobby Love was a family man. Bobby Love was a deacon at his church. Every Sunday our pastor would preach about forgetting the past, and forgiving ourselves, and looking ahead. And that's exactly what I was doing. That part of my life was buried back in North Carolina. And it wasn't coming back."

* * *

"There was a piece missing. All these years I loved my husband. And he loved me—but something was missing. First, he never liked to be in photographs. And he always thought people were watching him. But I just thought it was vanity. I kept saying: 'C'mon, Bobby. You aren't that exclusive.' But then there was the deeper stuff. We had some beautiful love making. But other than that, there wasn't much affection. Not many hugs. Not much cuddling. Not much communication. I could only get so close and he'd shut down. Sometimes, when we were arguing, I'd be pouring myself out to him. And he'd just sit there with a scowl on his face. I thought it was me. I kept thinking: 'Maybe he doesn't want to be here.' But Bobby was a provider. He was always working two or three jobs. He'd cook, and do laundry, and spend time with the kids. I thought to myself: 'Everyone is different. People have different upbringings. This might be how Bobby shows love.' But it was hard. It wore me down. I cried so many tears about it. I remember during Christmas of 2014, I was on my knees in church, saying: 'Lord, please, I can't do this anymore.' I begged God to change my husband's heart. I'd reached the end of my rope. That was a few weeks before everything went down."

* * *

"My world came crashing down. Bobby's arrest was all over the papers. It seemed like the whole city was laughing at me. People at church would pull me aside, and whisper: 'You knew about this right? You had to know.' But I never knew. Forty years of marriage, four grown children, and I never knew. How could I be so stupid? I wanted to hide. I wanted to disappear. When I went to work that first day, everyone was gathered around the front desk. And they got real quiet when I walked in. But I told them: 'Don't just stand there. I need some love. Give me some hugs.' Of course I was embarrassed, but I was more hurt than anything. Bobby had deceived me for all those years. There was no truth in our house. I'm walking past this man every single day. We laughing. We joking. And he's not telling me anything? I was so angry. But I never hated him. I wanted to comfort him. I wanted to hold his hand. I told Bobby later, 'That's how I knew I loved you. Because even in the worst of it, I was thinking about you.' When I first visited him in prison, he broke down crying. His head was in his hands, and he told me: 'I know, you're going to leave me.' I told him: 'No Bobby Love, I married you for better or for worse. And right now this is the worst.'"

* * *

"I got to work. I wrote letters to the governor. I wrote letters to Obama. I gathered testimonials from everyone that Bobby ever knew: all the kids he used to coach, all the people at our church, all of our family members. I testified on his behalf. I didn't know a thing about Walter Miller. But I told them all about Bobby Love. And the parole board took mercy. After a year in prison, they let him come home. The day after he was set free, I sat him down and asked: 'What is it? Are we the Loves? Or are we the Millers?' And he said: 'We Love. We Love.' So I had him change his name legally. And now we're moving on. I still have my resentments. When we get in a fight, I'll think: 'This man better appreciate that I forgave him.' But the thing is-- I did forgive him. And when I made that decision, I had to accept all the territory that came with it. I can't make him feel that debt every day of his life. Because that's not the marriage I want to be in. The whole world knows now. We've got no secrets. But I think this whole mess was for the better of things: better for me, better for the kids, and better for Bobby. He doesn't have to hide anymore. He can look at me when I'm speaking. Not only that, he's hearing me too. My voice is heard. I used to walk on eggshells. I used to just go along. But I told him one thing. I said: 'Bobby, I'll take you back. But I'm not taking a backseat to you no more.' Because I got my own story to tell. I can write a book too. I might not have escaped from prison, and started a whole new life, and hid it from my family. But I forgave the man who did."

CHAPTER II

It's Not All Roses

At ten weeks the blood test came back with markers for Down Syndrome. Then the next week we found out there were further complications. There was a grieving process for both of us. We had to realize that things were going to be different. I think it was harder for my husband, even though he didn't cry as much as me. Sometimes it's not as easy for men to show emotion. Women tend to band together. I joined so many mom groups. I talked through everything. My husband is a bit of a jock, so I kept sending him videos of Down Syndrome athletes.

I wanted him to get excited about the possibilities. We drove to the beach one weekend shortly after the diagnosis, and the entire ride we talked about the future. We talked about how much of our daughter is going to be like any other child. And how we can still be a family. We can still go to Disney World. We can still have adventures. When we arrived at the rental house, I put one of the ultrasound pictures on the fridge. That evening we were sitting on the beach, about to go back inside, when this little girl with Down Syndrome came walking up to us. She was wearing a Minnie Mouse bathing suit. She didn't say a word. She just stood there— smiling at us."

❋ ❋ ❋

"There was an eighty percent chance of miscarriage. I walked around every day not knowing if my daughter was still alive. Every two weeks I went to the doctor to check for a heartbeat. I always asked them to face the ultrasound screen away from me. I couldn't bear to look. At week twenty-two my placenta began to fail. I was hospitalized at week thirty. The blood flow through the umbilical cord had been reversed. The delivery took three days. Her heartbeat was dropping. The chance of stillbirth was so high. During the emergency C-section, there were thirty people in the room. My husband said that all of them had an 'oh fuck' look on their face. The last thing I remember is the gas mask being put over my mouth. Then I woke up asking for milkshakes. They wheeled my entire bed into the NICU to meet my daughter. She'd had oxygen deprivation. Her heart was halfway beating. I was still paralyzed so I couldn't even sit up to look at her. The nurse took my phone, held it over my daughter, and turned it on 'selfie mode.' This is what she looked like when I saw her for the first time."

❋ ❋ ❋

"My maternity leave was spent bouncing between hospitals, therapists, and the insurance company. I still talk to a doctor every single day of every single week. My daughter has had five surgeries already—two on her heart. I have to fight so much. It took a month of phone calls with the insurance company just to get her a single shot that she needs to stay alive. I hear other parents say it's going too quickly. But it's not for me. We live in a different world. My kid doesn't babble. Doesn't eat food. Doesn't crawl. My husband is lucky because he has no idea what the milestones are supposed to be. But I do. I know what a fifteen-month-old should be able to do. Every month I have a mom's lunch with coworkers. They're the most fantastic people in the world. But it's so hard to hear them complain that their kids follow them around and eat everything. My daughter has a feeding tube and doesn't move. Both my husband and I work full time. We're so tired. It's like a bucket that's being drained from so many holes. But you know what? It's better than the unknown. It's better than I imagined it was going to be. Because I'm a parent now. And when you're imagining all these things, it's so hard to picture the love. She's such a happy baby. She gets so proud of herself when she accomplishes something. She never wakes up crying. The one thing that comes easy to her in life is love and happiness."

❋ ❋ ❋

"Even within the Down Syndrome community, it can be hard to not compare. You've found a group of people going through the same thing as you. And suddenly there are gradations. I follow all these people on Instagram that are my age and have Down Syndrome babies. And it's easy to feel jealous. There are so many differing abilities. Some kids are already walking by now. Then there are the people with Down Syndrome who are revered. Some have testified before Congress. Some are models, and gymnasts, and mothers. And that represents hope for a lot of people. But that's also not the reality for a lot of people. And that hope can be devastating. What if your kid can't do those things? What if your kid can't do Special Olympics? But I'm optimistic by nature. And the only thing I truly need is that she'll have people who love her. And I mean people who aren't blood. I want her to be included and have friends and have a community. I want people to say 'hi,' and sit with her, and include her. If no boy asks her to prom, I'm going to be devastated. Because I imagine my own life without friends or social connections and it's so sad. I can't watch her go through that. And the hardest thing is that these are things I can't control. All of these experiences are so dependent on other people. I'll never be able to control how other people see her."

CHAPTER III

Hot Young Stud

Tanqueray, Tanqueray, Tanqueray. When this photo was taken, ten thousand men in New York City knew that name. My signature meant something to them. They'd line up around the block whenever I was dancing in Times Square, just so I could sign the cover of their nudie magazine. I'd always write: 'You were the best I ever had.' Or some stupid shit like that. Something to make them smile for a second. Something to make them feel like they'd gotten to know me. Then they'd pay their twenty bucks, and go sit in the dark, and wait for the show to start. They'd roll that magazine up tight and think about their wives, or their work, or some of their other problems. And they'd wait for the lights to come up. Wait for Tanqueray to step out on stage and take it all away for eighteen minutes. Eighteen minutes. That's how long you've got to hold 'em. For eighteen minutes you've got to make them forget that they're getting older. And that they aren't where they want to be in life. And that it's probably too late to do much about it. It's only eighteen minutes. Not long at all. But there's a way to make it seem like forever. I always danced to the blues. Cause it's funky and you don't have to move fast. You can really zero in on a guy. So that it seems like you're dancing just for him. You look him right in the eyes. Smile at him. Wink. Put a finger in your mouth and lick it a little bit. Make sure you wear plenty of lip gloss so your lips are very, very shiny. If you're doing it right, you can make him think: 'Wow, she's dancing just for me.' You can make him think he's doing something to your insides. You can make him fall in love. Then when the music stops, you step off the stage, and beat it back to the dressing room."

✳ ✳ ✳

"I grew up an hour outside of Albany. The neighborhood wasn't too nice, but it was better than the black neighborhood on Hill Street. Right now the house looks like shit, but back then it was completely clean. And my job was to keep it that way. My mother would come home after work and run her hand along the dining room table. Then she'd look at the tip of her finger. If she saw a speck of dust, she'd beat me with a belt. I hated that woman. The only thing I liked about her was her style. She looked just like the movie star Lena Horne. And whenever she walked down the street, both men and women would stop and stare. There used to be a store in downtown Albany called Flah's. And in the 1940's if you didn't buy your clothes from Flah's-- you weren't affluent. My mother only shopped at Flah's. She bought the best of everything:

silk blouses, thirteen pairs of shoes, a hat for every day of the week. No matter how much I hated her—and I hated her – I always wanted to dress like her. My mother might have been the only black woman in the capitol that wasn't working as a secretary. She was special assistant to the Governor. I've always wondered how she rose that high-- but I certainly have my guesses. She fit in so well with white society that she wanted nothing to do with anything black. She never acted black. She never talked black. She talked about blacks, but never talked black. She used to tell me that I'd be a lot prettier if she'd married someone with lighter skin. And you know what else she tried to tell me once? She was crying about something, and she tried to tell me that she never wanted kids. But she had me anyway so that she could have some-one to love. I looked at her like she was crazy. Cause she never showed me love. Not once. The only time we spent together was when I took ballet. I was on pointe at six years old. They won't even let kids do that anymore. My mother came to all of my les-sons and danced right alongside me. It was the only time we ever bonded. But she couldn't do pointe. Not even close."

❊ ❊ ❊

"I was the fly in a bucket of buttermilk. All my neighbors were Italians and Jews. My first crush was a boy named Neil Murray. He's fat and bald now, but back then he looked like a Kennedy. Every day he'd carry my books home from school. Until one day the nuns gave us a lecture about how you can't be interracial, so that stopped real quick. But I did everything else the white kids did: ice skating, snow skiing, horseback riding. My mother sent me to a private Catholic school, and we were reading all those classic novels: The Illiad, The Oddysey, Tale of Two Cities, all that stuff. We even studied Latin. No black kids were taking Latin in the 1940's, but I was near the top of my class. Every time there was an art thing going down, the teachers would put me right in the middle of it. One Christmas they put me inside a big refrigerator box, and wrapped it up in wrapping paper. All the parents gathered around. Then the music started, and the box opened up, and there I was-- dressed like a doll. Standing on pointe. I began to dance, and the parents went crazy. My mom was so proud that day. Because none of the other kids could do it, even though they were white. Sometimes on the weekends I'd go over to these kids' houses, and they had families like you'd see on television. Everyone would be talking nice. Like they were happy to be together. Even the dog would be wagging its tail. But there was nothing like that in my house. My parents didn't even sleep in the same bedroom. There were no hugs or kisses. My only friends were my dolls. At night I'd pull a blanket over the top of an old card table and pretend it was my home. I'd be under that table, with all my dolls, in their beautiful dresses, and it was like I had a little family. I'd gather them real close and we'd say a prayer: "Lord, please get me out of here so I can find a family that loves me." I'd say it over and over. "Lord, please get me out of here so I can find a family that loves me." One night my mother must have heard me in the hallway, because she burst into my room. She kicked over that card table and slapped me across the face. When I came home from school the next day, all my dolls were gone."

✽ ✽ ✽

"All I ever thought about was getting out of that house. I'd spend hours watching those old black-and white Hollywood musicals-- with Esther Williams doing ballet in the water. She'd be surrounded by rows and rows of smiling white women, kicking their legs high in the air. I'd fantasize about running away from home and dancing right alongside them. That's the problem with growing up in a white world. You think you can do anything that white people can do. By the time I was a teenager, the only black person I knew was an old lady at our church. I didn't know anything about black culture. I didn't know anything about black music. I had an entire record collection, and my favorite album was Rhapsody in

Blue-- that's how white I was. I began to feel like I didn't belong, which is probably why I fell in love with the first black guy who would talk to me. His name was Birdie. And he was from the hood, but he didn't act like a hood guy. He had a car. He took me places. I don't remember much else about him. I just remember that he told me he loved me-- which I believed cause I was stupid. I didn't know what the fuck love was. I was all alone. There was nobody to discuss girly stuff with: this happened, that happened, none of that stuff. So when Birdie told me that all I had to do was pee after sex, I believed him. And you can guess what happened. Three months later I was pregnant. I knew my mother was going to kill me. But Birdie came to my house, and showed her this big, fake diamond ring. He spun this story about how he was going to bring me to New York and give me this great life. My mother actually seemed impressed. I think she was happy to be getting rid of me. And I was excited too. The plan was for Birdie to go ahead to New York and find us an apartment. I'd drop out of school and follow behind a few weeks later. I remember arriving in Penn Station, four months pregnant, thinking I was about to have The American Dream. Birdie showed up with flowers in his hand. Then he gave me a kiss and told me to go back upstate. Turns out he was already married, and his wife was some sort of invalid, so he decided that he couldn't leave her. I was shit out of luck."

"I knew my mother wasn't going to let me come back home. So I decided to leave Albany for good. I was gonna go to New York and live a fantasy life like Esther Williams, with music and dancing and smiling people all around me. But first I needed to sneak back into my bedroom and get the rest of my clothes. I waited until late at night, when everyone was asleep, and I climbed inside the window. I started filling up my bag with all my dolls and my clothes. And I almost made it. I was just about to climb back out. When suddenly the lights flicked on and there was my mother—

standing in her bathrobe, madder than hell. She called the cops and had me arrested for burglary. The judge gave me a choice. Either I could give the baby up for adoption, and go back to live with my mother-- or I could do 'one to three' in Bedford Hills prison. I agreed to give the baby up. But I wasn't going back to my mother's. So I told the judge to send me to prison. The whole courtroom gasped. Three weeks later my son was born. The hospital sent him straight to St. Margaret's Children's Home, and I was shipped off to Bedford Hills. It was a modern prison. There weren't bars on the cells or anything. But I was scared. I was only eighteen. I'd never been around criminals before. Since nobody from the outside was putting money into my account, I had to get a job in the prison factory. Back in the day all the bras and underpants were made by convicts—so that's what we were doing. I'd always been good at art, so on the side I started making marriage certificates for all the lesbians. I'd use crayons to draw little hearts and stuff. Then I'd sign it at the bottom to make it look official. In return they'd give me cigarettes—which was money. Pretty soon I had a little reputation. I was like the artist of the prison. The warden even asked me to choreograph a dance for the prisoners on family day. Nobody had any problems with me. I was certain that I'd get paroled after nine months. But on the day before my interview, the warden called me into her office. 'I've got some bad news,' she said. 'Your mother is fucking the head of the parole board."

❋ ❋ ❋

"The warden knew that the fix was in. She told me that my parole would be denied. But she was cool. She knew I didn't belong in prison. So she told me that if I could wait one more month, the head of parole would on be on rotation at the men's prison in Dannemora. Then she drew up some fake papers and claimed that I was locked up in solitary. My board hearing got rescheduled—and the next month I went in front of a whole new panel. My test scores were off the chart. I was like the valedictorian of the prison. And the warden even wrote me a letter of recommendation, so my parole was approved. I knew just what I was going to do. I was never going back to Albany. I was going to catch the first bus to New York City, and begin a brand new life. But before I left prison, there was one more thing I wanted to do. There was a white-haired woman named Roberta who lived on my wing. She came from Poughkeepsie Mental Hospital, and everyone was kinda scared of her because she had these bad dreams at night and screamed like her whole body was on fire. But she was also kinda famous for reading palms. So the night before I got released, I let her read me. I gave her my last cigarette, and she looked at my hand and started describing all these things. She told me that I'd live my entire life in New York City. And I'd only be in love once. And that it would be a tough life. And a lonely life. But that one day a lot of people would know my name. And the craziest shit about it, is that every single thing came true. Well, almost everything. Roberta told me that I'd come into some real big money one day. And that better happen quick. Cause I'm already 76."

❋ ❋ ❋

"I arrived in New York City on Valentine's Day. It was like being reborn. All my mistakes in life: the pregnancy, the prison time, everything—had been because I was trying to get away from something. But I was finally where I wanted to be. Now my mistakes would be my own. The first thing I did was get a room at the Salvation Army. I had nothing in my bag but $90, a pack of baby powder, and a bar of prison soap. My roommate was a prostitute named Edna, and she had the exact same bar of soap as me. But neither of us are admitting that we just got out of prison. I started working at a clothing factory off Washington Square. We were making waiter jackets or something. At first I was just cutting threads off stuff, but when the owner found out I could work an industrial sewing machine—he moved me up quick. On my days off I'd go out and explore the city. Back then a subway ride cost fifteen cents, but I always took the bus. Because I wanted to see everything: every park, every square, every skyscraper. There was none of this stuff in Albany. I'd always get off on the corner of 59th and 5th and watch the wealthy people walk down the street. Every single one of these women dressed like my mother. There was real money in New York. We had money back in Albany, but it always seemed like pretend money. Like everything was a 'put on.' If a person in Albany had a really nice ring, it was usually to distract you from the polyester they were wearing. But I can read fabric. So I knew the truth. And when you're really rich, everything reads money. That's how it was in New York-- money from head to toe. Leather all the way to the floor. One of the first things I did was get my wardrobe together. I could never afford what these rich people were wearing—I did all my shopping at the discount store-- but I managed to get a little something going. I bought myself a hat for every day of the week, just like my mother. The rest of my clothes were pleather-- except for my shoes. People with money only wear leather shoes. So I saved up for three weeks and bought myself some brand new leather shoes."

* * *

"At night I'd lay in bed and listen to the sounds of the street. I never wanted to fall asleep, because I didn't want to dream about my mother screaming at me. So I'd listen to all the noise outside and I'd start to feel like I was missing out on something. That's how New York sounds late at night, when you're lying in bed and you're scared of going back to where you came from. It sounds like you're going to lose your place in line. And if you don't get out of bed—the thing that was supposed to happen to you is gonna happen to someone else. I'd make myself so nervous thinking like that, I'd put on my leather shoes and hop an uptown bus to Times Square. I'd walk down Broadway past all the theaters, and dream about dancing there one day. Then I'd walk a little bit further, past the adult theaters— where I actually end up dancing. By the end of the night I'd usually find myself in one of the clubs. The most famous club in Times Square was the Peppermint Lounge. It's a parking garage now, but back in the day it was the place to go if you wanted to hear some music. That's where Chubby Checker invented the twist. But it was usually filled with tourists, so I spent most of my time across the street at The Wagon Wheel. It was more like a community. The clubs weren't like they are today. There was no VIP section. No velvet ropes and champagne service. Everyone mingled: the pimps, the hustlers, the entertainers, the tourists. Back in the sixties, every club in New York was putting in a stage for GoGo dancers, because a Gogo club could make twice as much as a regular club. The girls would dance in cages or behind the bar, and guys would line up to put money in the jukebox. These girls were getting paid. On a busy night they could make $100 in tips during a five-hour shift. I had to work a full month at the factory for that kind of money. And I was a better dancer than all of them. But I knew the clubs wouldn't hire me. Because Gogo Dancers had to be perfect. They couldn't have stretch marks. Couldn't have tattoos. And they couldn't be black."

❋ ❋ ❋

"When you go to the clubs every night, you start to see the same people. They'd buy me drinks. They'd ask me to dance. It was like a make-believe family for me. I never knew much about these people. Maybe they had real families. Maybe they weren't alone as me—but they never made me feel that way. They accepted me. They called me 'Black Stephanie.' I got along with everybody:

the pimps, the hustlers, the drug dealers, the mob guys. Especially the mob guys. Every single one of them had a black woman on the side, so they'd flirt with me all the time. And I had no problem with it. They dressed their asses off. They talked romantic. It wasn't long before I was hanging with a whole crew of Italians. And they started giving me little side jobs so I could earn some extra cash. My steadiest work came from a guy named Joe Dorsey. He was the best thief in the city, but he didn't look like what he did. He looked like Wall Street. His fingernails were always perfect. And his wife was an upscale escort who wore designer clothes. Joe had one of the best hustles in town. Back in those days, rich women would keep their jewelry and mink coats locked up in storage until it was time for a big event. Then they'd always go to the beauty parlor and start bragging about their fancy parties, and all the nice things they were going to wear. Joe was paying off a hairdresser at the nicest parlor on Madison Avenue. And the moment these women started jabbing, she'd sneak away to call Joe Dorsey. All he ever needed was an address. Because Joe could get past any doorman, since he dressed like Wall Street. And he could pick any lock. So by the time these women got home, their whole place had been looted. My job was to sell the mink coats. I'd wear them to all the clubs and wait until I got a compliment. Then I'd unload it. Joe gave me a commission, plus I always added an extra ten percent to his price. So I was making money on both ends."

✳ ✳ ✳

"One of my best customers was a GoGo dancer named Vicki. Vicki was a blonde-haired, blue-eyed bombshell. She worked the Peppermint Lounge when it was really going, but she made a lot of money on the side as an upscale call girl. All her clients came through a woman named Madame Blanche. Blanche controlled the high-end prostitution in the city. All the powerful men came to her because they knew she wouldn't talk. But that didn't mean

Vicki wouldn't talk. Vicki told me everything. One night I was selling her a coat, and she told me that Madame Blanche was looking for a black girl. The client was Alfred Bloomingdale—the owner of the department store. It was a role play thing. All I had to do was go to his hotel room and pretend to be a maid. She promised me that I wouldn't even have to take off my clothes. And the pay was $300-- so I agreed. Bloomingdale was set up in a permanent suite at a fancy hotel off Park Avenue. When I walked in the door, he was lying in the bed, wearing one of those smoking jackets like Hugh Hefner wears. He was surrounded by five white hookers in French lingerie. They weren't even touching him. They were just sorta sitting on the edge of the bed, looking bored. On the bedside table there were stacks of $100 bills. He peeled off three of them and handed them to me. Vicki had coached me so I knew what to do. He ordered me around for awhile. I was serving them drinks, and picking up clothes off the floor. He gradually got more and more demanding, and I was saying dumb stuff like: 'Yessuh, Mr. Bloomingdale. Oh Yes, Mr. Bloomingdale.' But after thirty minutes I was supposed to switch it up. The plan was for me to start talking back, and he was going to get angry and call me the N word and whip me with his necktie. I didn't care. I was getting $300. But when that time came, he didn't grab a necktie. He grabbed a leather belt. And that wasn't in the agreement. So I grabbed my coat and got the fuck out of there. Thankfully I got my money up front."

* * *

"One weekend the Temptations came into town to play a show at the Copacabana. Nobody black had ever performed there, so everyone was buzzing about it. At the time Vicki was fooling around with one of the singers, so she asked me if I wanted to come out and party with them. I told her 'no problem.' It didn't seem like a big deal to me. Vicki was obsessed with famous people and their money, but I could care less. The way I saw it: it wasn't my fame. And it wasn't my money. So why would I care? We made a plan to meet at BB Kings—the original location in the basement of the Americana Hotel. All of The Temptations were there, but I got paired off with Dennis—who happened to be the finest of them all. We had the best table in the house. And I could tell that Dennis was into me. We were flirting and laughing. Everyone was having a great time, when all of the sudden James Brown comes walking up to our table. He must have been drinking. Because he pulled up a chair, and started jabbing his finger at Vicki, screaming about how The Temptations had no business being with a white woman. He kept saying that there were plenty of sisters who look good. Now I'm listening to all this 'black and proud' shit, and I'm getting pissed. Because James Brown was keeping a white girl named Geri Miller in the Knickerbocker Hotel. I knew it for a fact. Everybody knew it. James had gotten her a floor length fox coat for Christmas, and every time he got mad at her-- he took it back. It was a big joke in the clubs. So I sat there quietly until James was finished with his ranting and raving, then I said: 'Excuse me Mr. Brown, but Geri Miller would like her coat back.' James looked at me like he needed to take a shit. He didn't say a word. He just slammed some money down on the table and walked out. The Temps started laughing so hard that they were rolling on the floor. And when it was time to leave-- they invited us back to their hotel room."

* * *

"The Temps were staying at some fancy hotel off Central Park South. Right when we walked in the door, Vicki started sitting in her man's lap, and he's kissing on her neck. So Dennis starts doing the same thing. I knew what he was expecting to happen, but I don't do one-night stands. So I'm giving him nothing back. After twenty minutes he got tired of trying, so he gets up and disappears into his bedroom. I thought he'd gone to sleep. But ten minutes later he walks back in, and he's wearing nothing but a leopard silk bathrobe. It was tied so loose that he was just swinging in the breeze. And I mean swinging low. Like you wouldn't believe. Nice to look at – but no thank you. I had a shift at the factory early the next morning, so I looked at my watch and said: 'I gotta get out of here.' On the way out I could hear all the other Temps laughing. It was probably the only time that man had ever gotten turned down. And ever since that night, every time the Temptations came to town—I'd go to the show. This went on for decades. And always on my way out the door, I'd tip the stagehand to pass a note to Dennis: 'Do you still have that leopard bathrobe?' I must have passed him thirty different notes over the years. I knew it was driving him crazy. The last time I saw him was a few years back at a club downtown. By then he was potbellied but he could still sing his ass off. I got myself a table right up front, and the whole show he was singing straight to me. Both of us looked so different. There was no way he could recognize me. But during the intermission, I passed the same note that I always do. And when he came back out—he was still singing straight to me. There was one more concert scheduled for later that year in Queens. I'd made up my mind that I was finally going to reveal myself. But he ended up getting sick, and he passed away before I ever had the chance."

* * *

"After a few months in New York I was finally starting to get a little something together. I managed to save enough money to get my own room at the Times Square Hotel. It was just a sink and a bed and a radiator, but it felt like The Plaza to me. For the first time in my life, I could close the door at night and relax for a second. But that didn't last for long. One morning the owner of the factory called me into his office. I thought I was getting a promotion. But he closed the door behind me and said: 'Here's how it's going to work. Either you sleep with me, or I'll give a bad report to your parole officer, and you'll go back to jail.' This was some old, scroungy looking white guy. Exactly what you'd imagine a factory owner to look like. And I'm not saying I would have fucked him if he was any younger—but you've got to be kidding me. So I told him where to put it. I walked out of his office feeling good. I felt like I had some power. But that only lasted for three minutes, because I remembered I was living at the Times Square Hotel and rent was due next week. At the club that night, I started telling Vicki about my problems. She reached into her purse and pulled out a clipping from the Village Voice. It was an ad from a talent agency-- holding auditions for GoGo Dancers. 'They'll never know you're black on the phone,' she said. 'give them a call.' And she was right. They asked my cup size. And my measurements. But they never asked if I was white. I practiced all week for my audition. Most GoGo Dancers wore the same ballroom shoes that the Rockettes were wearing, but I could dance in heels. So I bought myself some bright red five-inch heels. And the moment I walked in the door, the guy's jaw nearly dropped to the floor. I was the blackest thing in the world. I think he'd already made up his mind that he was going to tell me 'no.' But I put on some BB King and started to dance. And I knew just how to do it. All slow and sensuous. Not like they do in Harlem. Like they do downtown. And when the music finally stopped, he was quiet for a few seconds. Then he stood up, smoothed out his pants, and said 'I think we can work something out.'"

✳ ✳ ✳

"My first steady gig was at a bar called Billy's. I danced there every Wednesday night with a brunette named Lisa. Back in the day there was a famous advertisement for Chesterfield Cigarettes, showing nothing but a pair of legs in fishnet stockings. Lisa was those legs. Her customers used to fold bills and tent them on the bar. And Lisa would crouch down slowly, unhook one side of her

G-string-- just enough to pick up the bill-- then stand back up. It didn't take me long to notice that Lisa was getting ten-dollar tips, and I was only getting a dollar. So I practiced that trick over and over again, until I could do it without falling down. After a few months I built up a little reputation for myself. That's how it works when you're a go-go dancer. You work a particular place, on a particular day, and you start to get a following. If I worked Monday at a club, I worked Monday forever. Because my customers kept coming back. The other girls would ask questions to figure out if a guy was worth their time. They'd ask about his apartment. Or his car. When the 212-area code came out for Manhattan, a lot of the girls were even asking for phone numbers. But I never asked those questions. Rich, poor, skinny, fat—I treated everyone the same. My most loyal follower was an auto mechanic named Oscar. For years he came to every one of my shows. No matter where I danced, he'd show up in his greasy uniform. Oscar's wife had abandoned him, and he was raising three kids on his own. Sometimes he'd stay until closing time and we'd get to talking about our problems. But he never hit on me or anything-- he'd just give me advice and stuff. And I always listened. Because the way I saw it—if you're raising three kids on your own, and you're getting through it, I'll listen how you're getting through it. Oscar was a lonely guy. He used to save up silver dollars all year long, then on Christmas he'd glue them to the outside of chocolate boxes and give them to his favorite dancers. A lot of the girls laughed at him behind his back. But I really cared for Oscar. He was a great father to those kids. I kept the boxes that he gave me, and I never even spent those silver dollars."

* * *

"Carmine walked into my life on New Years Eve. I was dancing somewhere. Some place in Midtown—who knows. And he walked in with a group of friends. Everyone dresses on New Years

Eve, but he stood out. He looked like Franki Valli. I remember thinking it was weird that he didn't have a date. Carmine had a job at the General Motors factory, but he didn't dress blue collar. He dressed like a Guido. Silk tie. Pressed shirt from The Custom Shop. French cuffs with cuff links. And perfect hair. Later on when we were fucking, I'd always try to grab his hair. And he'd say: 'Please, Steph! Not the hair! Not the hair!' But I didn't even talk to him that first night. I might have smiled at him. But I smiled at everybody. So I'm not sure why he kept coming back. He started showing up whenever I danced. He was always alone. And he always dressed perfectly. It was against the rules for customers to flirt with the girls—so I don't even remember how we started talking. But he was charming. He made me laugh. He didn't have any college, but he never sounded stupid. I started to have a little crush on him. One night he got the owner's permission to ask me out. And when I stepped off the stage, he offered to buy me dinner at any restaurant in Times Square. I chose Howard Johnson's. I was a cheap date. I ordered the fried clam sandwich. I don't remember what we talked about, but we started going out all the time after that. Carmine was always with me. I'd take him to the clubs on my nights off, and everybody was crazy about him. He even got along with the pimps. He could talk to anyone. And that boy could dance. We used to joke that Carmine had some black in him, because he had such good rhythm. All these women would try to pick him up because they didn't know he was with me. And I wasn't one to stop him. He never stopped me either. I could talk to anybody. I could dance with anybody: fast dance, slow dance, it didn't matter. That's one thing I loved about Carmine. I always had my freedom."

❋ ❋ ❋

"Carmine used to keep a blanket in the back of his convertible. Some nights, instead of going home, we'd pick up two sandwiches from Smiley's and take them out to Central Park. We'd lay the blanket out in Sheep's Meadow and have sex. Then we'd just sit there talking until the sun came up. One night I was telling him a story about the only vacation I'd ever been on. My mother had taken me to Cape Cod to visit my 'long lost Uncle Pete.' It was really just some guy she was fucking on the side—but I got a free trip out of the deal. When I finished telling him the story, Carmine turned to me and said: 'Do you want to go now?' I thought he was making a joke, so I kinda laughed. But he got real serious and asked me again. We ran back to his convertible and drove all night. We didn't have a hotel or anything. We just laid our blanket out on the beach and waited for the sun to come up. We were the only two people out there. And I don't know why, but I started telling him things that I'd never told anyone before. I told him all the things I'd been hiding from everyone else. I told him about my mother. And how she used to beat me. And how I still dreamed about her screaming at me. I told him about the pregnancy. And the prison time. And I told him that when I'm all alone, sometimes I feel like I don't even exist. When I was finished talking, I looked over, and I kinda expected him to not be there anymore. But he was still right there. We watched the sun come up over the ocean. I'd never seen anything like it before. I'd seen it in pictures, but I'd never really seen it. The water was the same color as the sky. Carmine had his arm around me, and I think it might have been the happiest I'd ever felt in my life."

* * *

"Carmine and I moved into an apartment on 34th Street. We knew they'd never rent to a black girl, so I sat in the car while he talked to the landlord. We celebrated that first night together by cooking hamburgers on the patio, then we decided to take a walk around the neighborhood. And I'm not sure who spotted it first—but there was a tractor trailer parked across the street with its door unlocked. Carmine popped open the back and found a whole load of Charles Jordan women's shoes. By the time we sold it all, there was enough to cover six-months rent. And we made sure to spread the wealth around. On the weekends we'd throw these huge parties and invite everyone from the club except for the pimps. Our friend Mickey drove a delivery truck for the New York Times, but on the side he sold coke to a lot of famous people. He used to show up at our parties with a punchbowl full of joints and a dinner plate full of cocaine. I never touched the stuff, but everyone else seemed to love it. Those parties went until 4 AM. At the end of the night we'd lay out blankets and people would fall asleep on the floor. It was nice having the same people around all the time. It started to feel like a real home. And Carmine treated me like I'd never been treated before. He bought me flowers. He took me places. We used to get dressed up every Friday night and get dinner in the Latin Quarter. And since so many of his friends were thieves, he was always bringing me presents. My favorite color is purple, so he got me a purple dress. He got me my first real diamond ring. And on my 25th birthday he got motorcycles for both of us. Every time we got in a fight and needed to cool off, we'd just go out riding. Those were the happiest days of my life. It felt like I finally had a little family. Of course Carmine could never tell his actual family about me. They'd kill him if they knew he was with a black girl. So every year he'd have two Christmas's. The one he spent at his parents' house in Jersey, and the one he spent at home with me."

❋ ❋ ❋

"Carmine was a hustler—but he was steady. Our bills were always paid, so I never had to dance much when I was with him. The only job I kept was at a place called The Metropol. It was a big, three-story club owned by a bunch of mob guys and one connected Is-raeli. And it was the best place in the city to dance go-go-- because they booked by the week and the place was always packed. There were a lot of office buildings around so the customers had money. And the stage was behind the bar so they wouldn't even try to touch you. We always had three girls dancing: two on the floor, and one doing sexy moves on a red velvet couch. Things got so hot on that couch that guys would sometimes try to jerk off at the bar. We called them 'shoulder jumpers.' Because even if they covered their lap with a coat, you could always see their shoulders jumping. A lot of my old followers couldn't afford the Metropol. But Oscar still came to every one of my shows. He wasn't allowed to wear his greasy uniform, but he still showed up. He'd always sit in the same seat. He'd order the same glass of Tanqueray. And every Christmas he'd give me the same chocolate box covered in silver dollars. Sometimes when my shift was over, Oscar and I would sit at the bar and talk for hours. He never hit on me once. He was the closest thing to a father figure that I ever had. He always picked up the phone when I called. One weekend Carmine was in Vegas, and I got diarrhea so bad that I couldn't get off the toilet. I called every single girl I knew. But nobody would come help me. Oscar drove all the way from Brooklyn to bring me a bottle of Imodium. He didn't even ask questions. That's how he was. He's the only one I could completely trust. I told him every-thing about my personal life. So he's the only one who knew that things had started going south with Carmine."

❋ ❋ ❋

"We'd been living on 34th Street for a few years when a prostitute moved into our building. Her name was Candy or something. And at first I thought Carmine was fucking her, because she kept knocking on our door. But one day the elevator wasn't working and I caught the two of them shooting up in the stairwell. Car-mine swore it was a one-time thing. But I started to notice little changes. He didn't want to go out much anymore. He kept dozing off on the couch. And then my tip money began to disappear. Later I'd find out that Carmine had been using for years. But I'd been too square to notice. He was the only junkie in the world who could keep a 9 to 5. And he was shooting up between his toes, so I never saw tracks on his arms. Everything seemed normal. I never had to tell him to do anything. It would always be: 'I'll wash the dishes tonight,' or whatever. Junkies don't do that. There wasn't much sex, I remember that. But he'd give me hugs. We'd watch TV together. So for the longest time I never knew. We tried a few programs after he finally came clean. But every time he went to rehab, he'd just meet another connection. Then he'd go straight back to the drugs. I couldn't handle the lies anymore. It was like I was living with someone who wasn't real. And everything he said was part of a script. I think Carmine sensed what was coming. Because every day he was asking me to marry him. And the worse he got on drugs, the more he asked. I'd always tell him no. It wasn't because I didn't love him— I loved that man more than I've ever loved another person. I just couldn't be with a junkie. It wasn't easy to leave. We didn't have any savings. And the apartment was in his name, so I had nowhere to go. At some point I figured in my crazy mind that if I married him, I could divorce him. And if I divorced him—at least I could keep the apartment. So the next time he proposed, I said 'yes.' We went to city hall. I wore a black dress because I knew it was the end. He didn't know, but I knew."

✳ ✳ ✳

"I still have the last Christmas Card that Carmine gave me. It was the Christmas he bought me fake tits. On the card he wrote: 'I hope our next five years together are better than the last five.' But we weren't even together for five weeks after that. I went to the courthouse and filed for divorce. I didn't want his money. I didn't want any of his stuff. I even gave him back the motorcycle, because I didn't want him to have any reason to come around. He started ringing my doorbell at all hours of the night. He was screaming outside my window. He was out of his mind on drugs, and I called the cops so much that they stopped responding. At the time I'd taken a second job working as a coat check at The Wagon Wheel, and that's where Carmine finally found me. He walked right past the bouncers because everyone knew him. He stood right in front of me. He looked like he'd been crying. Then he pulled a gun out of his coat, and pointed it at my face, and told me that he still loved me. I looked him right in the eyes. I didn't even say a word. But my knees were shaking so bad that I could barely stand up. The bouncers saw what was going on and they wrestled him to the floor. Then they threw him out on the street. But nobody called the police. Because everybody loved Carmine. That night I called Joe Dorsey and told him what happened. I wasn't selling coats for him anymore, but we were still friends. So he told me not to worry. I knew that Carmine scored his heroin at a burned-out apartment on 50th street. So Joe Dorsey and his goombas parked across the street, and rolled up on Carmine right after he scored. They told him that they could care less if he was Italian. And they didn't care if I was a black girl. If I ever fell down the stairs, or got a scratch on my face, they were gonna shoot him full of heroin and throw him in the river. He'd look like just another dead junkie. There wouldn't even be an investigation. Carmine stopped coming around after that."

✻ ✻ ✻

"Every once in a while when I was dancing, guys would ask me if I did bachelor parties. And I always said 'no,' because I knew they wanted me to strip. But I wasn't stupid. I knew that dancing wasn't going to last forever. So when things fell apart with Carmine, I started saying 'yes.' It was all about money. A good GoGo dancer could make $100 in tips over a four-hour shift. But burlesque paid $150, and your set only lasted eighteen minutes. My first gig was at a volunteer firehouse in Long Island. I was so nervous that I had to pee every five minutes. And I kept having to stop the performance while they drove away on calls. But I must have done something right, because they booked me again on the spot. And the captain drove me all the way back to New York with the siren going. I decided right then to make a career out of it. The first person I told was Oscar. We were having a drink one night, like we always did, and I told him I was thinking about doing burlesque. But there was only one problem: 'Stephanie' wasn't sexy enough for burlesque, so I needed a new name. Oscar tried to help me come up with ideas. He kept sipping on his drink, and thinking real hard, but nothing was coming. Then after a few minutes, he slammed his glass down on the table and said: 'Tanqueray.' It sounded perfect to me. But that was the last thing that Oscar ever gave me. The next month he quit taking his blood pressure medication because he wanted to get a hard on for a stripper named Crystal Blue. And he ended up having a stroke. He lived for a few weeks after that. He couldn't move much. And he could barely speak. But every day I visited him in the hospital. I put the word out to all the other girls, but none of them came. In the end I was the only one there. He started crying on the night before he died, because I think he knew he was close. And nobody had come to see him. All those years, all those chocolates, and all those silver dollars. They hadn't bought him a thing. He died completely alone."

✳ ✳ ✳

"Burlesque is a fancy sounding word, but it basically means stripping. You can wear a $3000 costume and strut across the stage like the Queen of England. But during the last number, you better be taking off your clothes. Every burlesque theater in Times Square had two types of dancers: house girls and features. The house girls work the same place every week, and they always come out first. They're just part of the crew. They don't have it, and nobody knows their name. It's the feature who fills the seats. She travels from venue to venue, and always closes the show. It's her name on the marquee. And she's the one getting paid. Now whenever I get into any kind of whatever-- I want to be the best. And Burlesque was no different. So naturally I wanted to be a feature. Only problem was there weren't no black features. But I was determined to cross the color line, because features were making $1000 a week—at least. The easiest way to become a feature was to work strong. Strong meant nasty. Dildos and stuff. And the stronger you worked, the more money you made. There was a girl named Monica Kennedy at The Melody Theater making $10,000 a week. You know how much ten grand a week was in the seventies--- cash? That's because Monica worked strong. She let it be known on the street that she douched with Listerine. And at the end of her act, the audience would form a single file line. Each guy would be given a hot dog bun, and Monica would shoot hot dogs out of her vajayjay-- right into those buns. She had mustard, relish, everything. Nobody left her show hungry. That's how you made $10,000. Cash. But I could never do it. So I had to figure out another way."

✳ ✳ ✳

"A lot of girls broke into the business by working with an agent. But that was an even dirtier path. The biggest agent in town was named Dick Richards. And if you worked with him, you had to have a ménage-a-trois with his girlfriend. I wouldn't do it. Plus I knew that Dick Richards would never give his best gigs to the black girl. So I needed another way to stand out. The first thing I tried was a snake. My cousin had gotten a six-foot snake from a pet store, then decided he didn't want it. So I made it part of my show. I would drape it around my shoulder every time I danced.

The snake thing worked OK for awhile, especially when I was performing in a theater. But whenever I was working the floor at a private party, all the guys would freak out. So I needed something different. My next idea was to swallow a sword. I took a trip to Tannen's, which was the biggest, most famous magic store in the world. It had everything for magic tricks: trick mirrors, trap doors, boxes where you could saw people in half. Back then the owner of the store was a guy named Tony, and I was honest with him. I told him I wanted to swallow a sword so I didn't have to shove dildos up my hoo-hah. That really killed him. He gave me a tour of the shop, and started introducing me to all the real magicians. He kept asking me to repeat what I'd told him. Eventually we found a fake sword that would roll up in my mouth, but then he had a better idea. He went into the back and brought out a little brown box. Then he opened it up, and pulled out a special trick. I'd never seen a trick like this before. It was the trick that put me on the map. In the 1970's, if you were a certain kind of guy, and you heard the name Tanqueray-- you thought of this trick."

✳ ✳ ✳

"I always saved my special magic trick for the grand finale. I'd bring it out during my final number, which was usually Donna Summer's Love To Love You Baby. The guys would start roaring as soon as the song came on, because they knew what was coming. By that time I'd be down to a silk negligee made from thirty yards of silk. And even though I was full nude, I could twirl that negligee so fast that you never saw a thing. There would always be two baby bottle tops covering my nipples. And right as Donna was hitting the high note—'I love to love you, babbbby' – I'd start tugging on those bottle tops, and chocolate milk would shoot out into the front row. It drove all the guys crazy. And I never let anyone near my equipment, so nobody could figure it out. There was a full-blown rumor in the community that black girls make chocolate milk. And I just let them run with it. Because my shows were always full. The minute the doors opened—the guys would be running for the front row. I worked my way up to feature in less than a year. Nobody had ever done that before. I was just like Jackie Robinson-- black number one. Make room for Tanqueray, cause here I come."

* * *

"The other dancers weren't too happy about my success. A lot of times they'd go out together after a show, but I was never invited. I didn't really fit in with them anyway. No offense—all of them were gorgeous. But they all had problems. I don't think any of them wanted to be doing what they were doing, so they were always drinking and snorting cocaine. My only friend in the community was a girl named Ronnie Bell. She was drop dead gorgeous. I mean next level. With or without make-up. All the other dancers were jealous of her—I'm not sure Ronnie realized it, but they were. Because she stole the show whenever she worked. This girl would have double gigs some nights. One show at eight. One show at ten. And the moment you saw her, you understood why. Ronnie had a tough childhood. She grew up in New Orleans, but she ran away from home at the age of fourteen to join the circus. Then she saved all that money and put herself through medical school. During the day she worked as a registered nurse. Ronnie never had to do any of it. She lived in a big house out in Queens. She only danced because she enjoyed it. That's why we got along so well—neither of us took ourselves seriously. We used to work a theater together outside of Fort Dix, where the black soldiers trained. I was always the feature. The promoter would lie and say I was 'Ms. Black Universe' or something. Ronnie and I used to meet at my apartment and drive out there together. As soon as we got on the Jersey turnpike, we'd take off our shirts, and wait for a big rig to come by and see us. It never took long because Ronnie was stacked. And I mean stacked. We had one of those CB radios in the car-- breaker nine or whatever. So we'd egg them on. And next thing you knew we'd have a convoy of tractor trailers escorting us down the highway. And when we finally got off the exit for Fort Dix, they'd all start honking their horns. TAH TAH TAH."

❋ ❋ ❋

"I could bring home $3000 a week if I was working the road. That was real money. Only the porn stars were making more than that, because nothing draws a crowd like having your face in a movie or magazine. In the 1970's-- the biggest porn star around was Gloria Leonard. She was like the Meryl Streep of porno. I used to work with her a lot. Whenever she had a new movie screening at Show World, I'd go along with her to warm up the crowd. But Gloria wasn't just a famous actress. She was the publisher of High Society, which was one of the biggest adult magazines going back then. Gloria was always trying to convince me to do a spread in her magazine, but I kept saying 'no.' Those shoots were full nude. But Gloria and I became good friends because she loved listening to my stories. One day we were laughing about something that happened, and she tells me: 'You'd make a lot more money if you wrote for me.' I told her: 'C'mon Gloria. It's all an act. My sex life is boring. There's nothing to write about.' That's when she leaned in real close, and whispered: 'It doesn't matter. Just make it up.' I went home that night and started typing. And when I showed Gloria what I wrote, she agreed to give me a column every other month. We called it Tattletales From Tanqueray. The pay was $500, and it only had to be two pages. The writing part took me forever because I'd failed typing class three times. But the ideas came easy. All I did was take a regular situation, and make it X-rated. I pretended like I was having sex everywhere: grocery stores, movie theaters, the DMV. I even wrote about having sex in prison. And people believed I was actually doing that shit. Gloria published everything I wrote. She said I was the only writer that they never had to edit. I still wouldn't let her put my picture in there--just the headshot. But it didn't matter. Because everybody read High Society. You couldn't buy that type of publicity. And after the first issues came out, I was like famous. Gloria would send boxes of the latest issue to all of my gigs. Guys would be lining up on the street to get a signature. And my salary went up-- big time."

* * *

"Everybody wanted a piece of Tanqueray. I was getting so many calls that I had to hire an answering service. Before long I had every account in the city. I mean everybody: the investment banks, the sports clubs, the unions, the masons. FDNY was my account. Transit was my account. I used to bring Ronnie with me every time I danced. We were having so much fun. I remember one night we were working the Friars Club together. They were roasting some television host that came on at 11:30, and this guy starts choking on a chicken bone in the middle of Ronnie's act. Somebody turned off the music and started screaming for help. Ronnie was a nurse, so she knew what to do. She yanked the guy out of his chair and did the Heimlich right there. He spit that chicken bone across the room, and Ronnie just went on with her show. We'd get $500 for every gig, and at the end of the night we'd split it down the middle. The NYPD was the only account we ever made pay up front, just in case the crap hit the fan and we needed to get out of there. Those parties were wild. All of them would be gambling and doing cocaine. After they cracked the Son of Sam case, I danced for one of the lead detectives. And he was dressed entirely in drag. Sometimes an entire precinct would rent out a boat on the Circle Line and ride up and down the Hudson all night. Ronnie and I would just set down a portable radio and get to work. The cops were great. They treated us like royalty. One night a rookie got so drunk that he threw Ronnie's costume into the Hudson. They stopped the entire boat, and made him jump in and get it for her. A lot of times those parties would go until 4 AM. And by the time we got back to Ronnie's house, we'd be so tired that I'd just spend the night. Her kids were asleep in the other room, so we'd always share the same bed. One time she rolled over and started rubbing up against me. I said: 'C'mon Ronnie, forget it. Don't even go there.' We never talked about it again. But there was nothing to talk about. I got it. She was lonely just like me."

❈ ❈ ❈

"Everything was fine when the music was playing. When people were laughing, and clapping, and shouting for more. But I knew I was tanking. Even when I was on the stage, and having fun—I was tanking. Some nights I'd go back to the dressing room, and look in the mirror, and I'd realize that I don't even exist. Nobody's clapping for Stephanie. They're clapping for Tanqueray. And sometimes I'd get so depressed thinking like that, I'd just start crying. I'd feel like running away and hiding from everyone. At least when I was a kid, I could crawl under the card table with my dolls. But that pretend shit wasn't working anymore. I was too old to fake like someone cared about me. But whenever I started to fall apart, I'd pull myself together and think about how lucky I was to be Tanqueray. At least I was successful. At least I had a career. At least when I'm Tanqueray, and I'm around people, I make them smile. I make them laugh with my stupid jokes. They're not trying to hurt me. But Tanqueray never came home with me. She always stayed out on the stage. It was Stephanie that walked out the back door, and nobody cared about her. Nobody except for Carmine. A few years after our divorce, he reached out through a mutual friend and asked if we could talk. They both came over to my apartment together. Carmine looked nice. A little older—but nice. He was dressed like the old days. He told me that he'd started a new life as a limo driver, and he wanted to work things out. He promised he was off the drugs. I listened to his whole speech, but then I told him that I wasn't sure. I was scared. I couldn't tell if he was on drugs or not. He seemed clean, but he had seemed clean when I was living with him. And if he started acting rough again—I had nobody to call. I didn't know any mob guys anymore. I think I told him that I needed a few days to think about it, and that I'd give him a call. But I knew I was never going to call him. As soon as the door closed, I fell on the floor and started to cry."

* * *

"I can't tell you the last time I danced burlesque. It wasn't some big thing. They don't throw you a retirement party at the Sheraton. The phone just stops ringing. It gets quieter and quieter until one week it's so quiet that you sorta decide you can make more money doing something else. If anything I was kinda happy about it. I could finally calm down on the make-up and start wearing dungarees. I remember the first thing I did was go out and buy a pair of loafers. But they didn't seem to fit right. I'd get this sharp pain in my leg every time I walked more than a few blocks. The doctor told me I'd been wearing heels for so long that my calf muscles were completely shrunken. And the only way to build them up again was to wear lower, and lower, and lower heels until I could walk without pain. I guess when you've been one way for so long, it's not easy to be something else. But I had no choice. There's no next step on the ladder when you're dancing for tips. The moment you step off that stage, you've got to start again at the bottom. So that's exactly what I did. But I wasn't worried. I'd been reinventing myself for my entire life. You wouldn't believe all the things I've done: I've managed a brothel, I've made adult baby clothes, I've done make-up for cross dressers. For three years I was one of the top dominatrixes in New York City. I have so many stories. Sometimes I'll remember the things that happened to me and I'll just start laughing. I hope when I get to heaven God shows me a movie of my life. But just the funny parts. Not the in-between parts, cause then we'd both start crying. Underneath all the laughs and the gags, it was always about one thing: survival. Tanqueray was a lot of fun. But Tanqueray was Stephanie. And Stephanie was a teenage runaway from Albany: doing what she needed to do, and being who she needed to be, to get what she needed to get."

* * *

"The city has changed so much. New York used to be a lot better. Maybe it was better cause I was younger. Or maybe it was better cause it was better. But it used to be better. I never really cried about it or anything. Every time the city changed, I just changed right along with it. But at some point things started changing too fast. Or maybe I got slower. I fell so far behind it was kind of like: 'What's the point?' There's no place to go anymore. The adult theaters are gone. The clubs are gone. Times Square doesn't even exist anymore. I mean, it's still there—but somebody figured out they could make a lot more money if they turned it into Disneyland, so that's exactly what they did. Now it's just billboards, and flashing lights, and some guy dressed up like the cookie monster. There isn't anywhere to go. There's nowhere to go that people can get to know each other. Or if there is a place to go—you need a corporate credit card just to afford a drink. And not everybody has it like that. What about the regular people? They used to have choices too. Maybe they were bad choices, but at least they were choices. For people looking to have a good time. And to forget about things. And to be less lonely for a second. Sure, New York is more family friendly now-- but not everyone has a family."

* * *

"Carmine ended up moving down to Florida to start a new life. Both of us dated a lot of other people, so there'd be long periods where we didn't talk. But we never lost touch. We even talked on the phone a few times last year. It was always about regular stuff. I never started crying, or said: 'I still love you,' or anything like that. We were getting too old for that movie shit. But we'd talk about things that happened. Sometimes we'd remember things differently, and we'd start arguing over who was right. But we'd always be laughing. Until one day he just stopped calling. I thought maybe I'd made him mad. Because the last time we spoke, I'd been joking about the time he got crabs in Vegas. But then weeks went by and I hadn't heard from him. So I started to think that maybe he was in jail or something. But one morning I typed his name on the Internet and found out that he passed away. His family was bringing him home to be buried in Newark. I wanted to go to the visitation, but I thought it would be kinda weird if I showed up. I'd be the fly in a bucket of buttermilk. So instead I lit a candle in my apartment and cried the whole afternoon. I still dream about him almost every night. And I still sleep with a teddy bear that he gave me. He was the only one who ever knew me. It wasn't always good—especially toward the end. But when I was with him I felt like I had a place. When I came home at night, there was somebody who actually wanted me to be there. And you can't just let go of something like that. Especially when you'd never felt it before. And you've never felt it since. Carmine was the only one who ever loved Stephanie."

❊ ❊ ❊

"I was walking down the street last winter. I don't remember what I was thinking about, but I was crying so I couldn't see much. And I slipped on a patch of ice. I wasn't on the ground for very long. Somebody rushed over and lifted me off the sidewalk-- but I haven't been able to walk since. Not much goes on in this apartment. Nothing really changes but the TV channels. So after awhile I started thinking that maybe the show was over for good. And to be honest I was kinda ready. It's not like I could go anywhere. And nobody was coming over to see me. It was starting to feel like everything that was going to happen to me had already happened. There was nothing left but a bunch of stories. And those aren't worth much when there's nobody to listen. But then I got this one last gig. Right as the curtain was coming down, I get this one last chance to be on stage. One last chance to be Tanqueray. And I haven't forgotten how to do it. Maybe I can't wear my heels anymore, but I can put on my make-up. And I might not be able to dance but I can talk like I need to talk. To make people smile. And laugh. And to keep them looking at me—so I can feel like I exist for just a few more minutes, before the lights go out for good. It's just a few minutes. That's how long you've got to hold em'. It's not very long at all. But if you're doing it right—it can feel like forever."

CHAPTER IV

Cherry Contact

I grew up in Russia. My mother was a severe alcoholic, so I spent my entire childhood in a home for troubled children. Some of the kids were violent. A lot of times there wasn't enough food. On the weekends my grandfather would pick me up and bring me to see my mom. But she was always so drunk that we'd never speak. I had plenty of opportunities to be adopted over the years. Families would visit the orphanage from all over the world. But I always said 'no.' Because my father was still alive. He was in prison but he was still alive, so I always imagined that eventually he'd come for me. Then one morning when I was nine years old, I woke up and my father was there to bring me home. It was the happiest moment of my life. I finally thought we'd be a family again. But my joy only lasted for a few days. Because he went back to doing criminal activity. He began to drink heavily. And soon he was beating my mother. After a few months he abandoned us and I went back to the orphanage. On Christmas Day they told me he was dead. After that I had nobody. My teacher became like a mother to me. Her name was Anna Mihailovna. I'd be a criminal without her. She brought me little gifts to comfort me. She encouraged me to read and paint. She showed me the right path. But she made me promise: 'The next time you have a chance to be adopted, you must accept.'"

* * *

"I remember it perfectly. They walked into our classroom while taking a tour of the school. They weren't even looking to adopt. Their friends had come to adopt one of my classmates, and they were merely tagging along. I was scared of them at first. But Anna nudged me to the front of the class. She encouraged me to give them one of my paintings. And the next day the orphanage director called me to her office. She said the Italian couple wanted to speak with me. They talked to me for an hour, and at the end they gave me a bag of oranges. I handed them out to all the other kids at the orphanage. I think the couple was touched by this, because that's when they invited me to visit Italy. Anna prepared all my documents. We visited for several weeks. They brought me all around Italy. I could tell they were friendly, but I was still frightened. They lived in such a big house. They were giving me so many things. And I couldn't understand a word they were saying. I had no idea why they cared about me so much. They told me they wanted me to stay and join their family. Anna begged me to do it. She told me that this was my chance to change my life. But I was so scared. All my friends were at the orphanage. So I told them 'no.' When I went back to Russia, I lost the backpack with their contact information. And I didn't see them again for fifteen years."

* * *

"My behavior grew worse over the years. I became a trouble-maker. I got in fights. And when I turned seventeen, the director kicked me out of the orphanage. Anna cried. She didn't want me to leave. But thankfully she'd prepared me well for life. She'd taught me to do little jobs like washing dishes and cleaning. She'd taught me right from wrong. She showed me affection. She knows what she did for me. She knows it was her. Every Christmas, every birthday, every women's day—I reach out and tell her that it was her. I joined the military after leaving the orphanage. After serving for a few years, I began working the nightshift in a bread factory. Things were going OK. It was a decent salary. I bought a car. But I wasn't moving forward in life. My first girlfriend dumped me. I fell into a dark place. Then one night I opened a very old book from my childhood, and a phone number fell out. It was the number of a young boy that I'd met during my trip to Italy."

* * *

"I called the number immediately. I didn't speak any Italian. But I kept repeating the names of the Italian couple, and I gave him my phone number. The couple called me back the next day with an interpreter. They told me they missed me. They said they'd been worried about me. I told them I was finally ready to change my life, and they said: 'Enough with Russia. Come live with us.' So I came to Florence. And when I arrived, they introduced me to everyone as their son. It was a whole new world. A whole new life. That first night my father sat me down, and he said: 'I understand you're afraid. But you're part of the family now.' I have a Mom and

Dad now. I have a brother and sister. I have aunts. I have uncles. We celebrate things together. I'd never celebrated Christmas before. I was twenty-three and I'd never even had a birthday cake. But now we celebrate all of these things. And we share sad things too. We go through things together. These last few years something deep down inside me has changed. I'm more open. I'm more caring. I don't really believe in God but there's got to be something. I don't know how any of this was possible. There is no one in the world like my mother and father. Now I want to enlarge our family. I want to have children of my own. And I want to tell them everything that happened to me."

CHAPTER V

Devil's Daughter

My childhood was dominated by her stories: living in the ghetto for two years, surviving off potato peels, running like an animal from the Nazis. She was the only one who survived. I have no grandparents. No aunts or uncles. Her entire family was killed. We rose up from the ashes. And my mother became a monster. She deprived us like she was deprived. My brother and I were always made to feel like a burden. Like we were leeching from her. There were no special occasions. No birthdays. No cake. Everything was counted. Everything was calculated. Whenever I asked for something, I was made to feel responsible for World War II. She'd say: 'I didn't survive Hitler to get you a bag of potato chips.' She never let me feel like we were in America. I felt like I was the one wearing stripes. I've dreamed about Hitler since I was child. He tells me I'm a mistake. And that I should have been killed. I remember when I grew older and started visiting the houses of friends. I saw how their parents treated them. How they were given gifts. And how they were loved. It felt like I was crawling out of the sewer, after the war, and learning that this entire time-- some people had been living normal lives."

❋ ❋ ❋

"My mother died on July 6th, 2005. One day toward the end of her life, we were in the subway together, carrying heavy packages, and I could see she was exhausted. She turned to me and said: 'A ganzeh leben is a schlep.' Which means: 'All of life is a schlep.' And for a moment I felt her pain. I realized I could still love her. She couldn't love me, but I could love her. Despite all the abuse she'd given me, I could feel her pain. I resurrected her old photo after her death. She's with her first husband. It was weeks before he was taken away. She's only twenty years old in that picture. That gorgeous face. That youth. How could I possibly hate her the same way? It's unfathomable. Not that she was right to be cruel, but it's unfathomable what she went through. I once helped her type a memoir to get reparations from the Germans. At the end of her story, she wrote: 'It was a life of horror. Having lost everything and everyone, I'd given up my struggle to live. And at that time, it would have been easier if they had killed me. But they didn't. So on I went, living in hell.'"

CHAPTER VI

A Touch Of Smile

My wife had been pushing to expand our family for eight years—but I kept resisting. I kept saying: 'What's wrong with you? We're almost done.' We were nearly forty years old. It was the second marriage for both of us. Our teenagers were about to graduate from high school. But she couldn't have children naturally, and there was always a deep yearning to adopt. She subscribed to a website called 'Rainbow Kids,' which featured children with special needs. She'd show me a profile from time to time. But I just couldn't do it. It seemed like too much work. Then one day in 2015 we had an outside speaker visit our office. He talked about his child with Down syndrome. And my heart was completely changed. I went home and told my wife the story. I was crying. She was crying. And I think both of us knew what was going to happen. A few days later she forwarded me an email from Rainbow Kids. The title was 'Magnificent Miles.' He was living in a Taiwanese orphanage. Just a beautiful little boy. Fifteen months old. Fluffy hair. And all alone. We knew it was our son."

❋ ❋ ❋

"The application process was a nightmare. It's like a messy divorce where they examine every little detail of your life. People try to scare the crap out of you about how emotionally damaged the kid will be. The agency made us sign a contract acknowledging fourteen ways the adoption could fall through—and there weren't any refunds. They warned it could take two years. And it's so expensive-- $32,000. But at that point Miles' picture was hanging all over our house. We talked about him all the time. He was already our son, but he was sitting in an orphanage. We needed to get him home as quickly as possible. I took out a loan against my retirement. I racked up so much credit card debt. I planned on using the reward points to buy his plane ticket home. Miles spent his second birthday at the orphanage. We filled a box with $300 worth of presents. It cost even more to ship. Inside we put his very first pair of walking shoes. Hip-hugger pants to help with his posture. A t-shirt that said: 'Someone in Fairfax, VA loves me.' And Mickey Mouse party favors for all the kids at the orphanage. Then we ordered him a cake from a local bakery. A few weeks later, the orphanage sent us a picture from the party."

❋ ❋ ❋

"We were extremely lucky. We completed the entire process in fourteen months and travelled to Taiwan on January 21st of 2017. The next morning we went straight to the orphanage. We sat in a waiting room on the ground floor, and after ten minutes they brought Miles around the corner. My wife dropped to her knees and hugged him like she'd never let him go. And of course that broke me down. I'm thinking 'Oh my God, this is my boy.' But when I went to pick him up, he started crying. I'm telling him: 'No, no, no! I'm Baba, I'm Baba.' But he didn't want me touching him. I went from the top of the world to the darkest valley. I tried playing with him. I tried getting him a Happy Meal. But he didn't want any of it. Nothing was going right. I felt so rejected. This went on for two days. Then on the third day we were sitting in our hotel room, and my wife left us alone while she took a shower. And all of the sudden this little boy started looking at me. And he had the biggest smile on his face."

❋ ❋ ❋

"It feels like Miles has been home forever. He's four years old now. He runs to me every time I open the door. He wants to play non-stop. He's the master of high-fives. He's the master of hugging the dog. He's also the master of needing attention while you're on the phone. Or when you just want to relax and watch TV for a second. But it always goes from frustrating to heartwarming in a second. Even though he can't express himself, he's amazingly empathetic. He's drawn to people who look alone.
There are meltdowns. And there are days when I feel like I'm not qualified for any of this. But on the days you don't think you can get through it— you don't realize that you're getting through it. And in the end, you're getting more than you ever give. Recently my wife started sending me pictures of other children, but I always said 'no.' Until I saw Mile's little sister for the first time. She's

from the same orphanage. Her name is Maddie. We submitted our papers three weeks ago."

ACKNOWLEDGEMENT

To my wonderful readers:I love you guys.

ABOUT THE AUTHOR

Kim Matos

For the past undisclosed amount of years, Kim Matos has been freelancing and designing blogs for small businesses.She lives in northern california with her dead fish larry and a bouncy bunny rabbit named Fred.

When she is not writting,she can be found picking up trash off the beaches,offering rides to the homeless and roastting her own coffee beans.